A [illegible] Teachers

Dorling Kindersley Readers is a compelling new reading programme [illegible] h leading [illegible] Honorary Fellow of [illegible]. Cliff Moon has spent [illegible] years as a teacher and teacher educator specializing in reading and has written more than than 140 books for children and teachers. He reviews regularly for teachers' journals.

Beautiful illustrations and superb full-colour photographs combine with engaging, easy-to-read stories to offer a fresh approach to each subject in the series. Each *Dorling Kindersley Reader* is guaranteed to capture a child's interest while developing his or her reading skills, general knowledge, and love of reading.

The four levels of *Dorling Kindersley Readers* are aimed at different reading abilities, enabling you to choose the books that are exactly right for each child:

Level 1 – Beginning to read
Level 2 – Beginning to read alone
Level 3 – Reading alone
Level 4 – Proficient readers

The "normal" age at which a child begins to read can be anywhere from three to eight years old, so these levels are intended only as a general guideline.

No matter which level you select, you can be sure that you are helping children learn to read, then read to learn!

www.dk.com

Project Editor Louise Pritchard
Art Editor Jill Plank

Senior Editor Linda Esposito
Senior Art Editor
Diane Thistlethwaite
Production Melanie Dowland
Picture Researcher
Andrea Sadler
Indexer Lynn Bresler
Illustrator Peter Dennis

Reading Consultant
Cliff Moon M.Ed.

Published in Great Britain by
Dorling Kindersley Limited
9 Henrietta Street
London WC2E 8PS

2 4 6 8 10 9 7 5 3 1

A CIP catalogue record for this book is available from the British Library

ISBN 0-7513-2862-6

Colour reproduction by Colourscan
Printed and bound in China by L.Rex Printing Co., Ltd.

The publisher would like to thank the following for their kind permission to reproduce their photgraphs:
c=centre; b=bottom; l=left; r=right; t=top

AKG London: 20; **Fortean Picture Library**: 17cr, 24tl, 28tl, 44tl; **Harry Price Collection, University of London**: 5, 22–23, 23tr; **Hulton Getty**: 11tr, 38clb; **Katz Pictures**: 34clb; **Mary Evans Picture Library**: 7tr, 18–19, 19tr, 19br, 21tr, 22tl, 22clb, 30bl, 36tl, 41tr, 43tr, 44–45, 46; **Peter Underwood**: 24cl, 24–25, 26; **Quadrant Picture Library**: Slick Shoots 12tl; **Robert Harding Picture Library**: Michael Short 6tl; Robert Francis 32tl; **South American Pictures**: Charlotte Lipson 47cr; **Tibet Images**: Ian Cumming 28clb; **Tony Stone Images**: Tony Craddock 18cl

Grateful thanks and acknowledgement to the following ghosthunters and spookbusters: Daniel Cohen, Michael Coleman, Joan Forman, John Fuller, Prof. Colin Gardner, Lorne Mason, John Masters, Ben Noakes, Edith Olivier, Harry Price, John & Anne Spencer, Colin Wilson

Contents

DORLING KINDERSLEY *READERS*
PROFICIENT 4 READERS

SPOOKY SPINECHILLERS

Written by Andrew Donkin

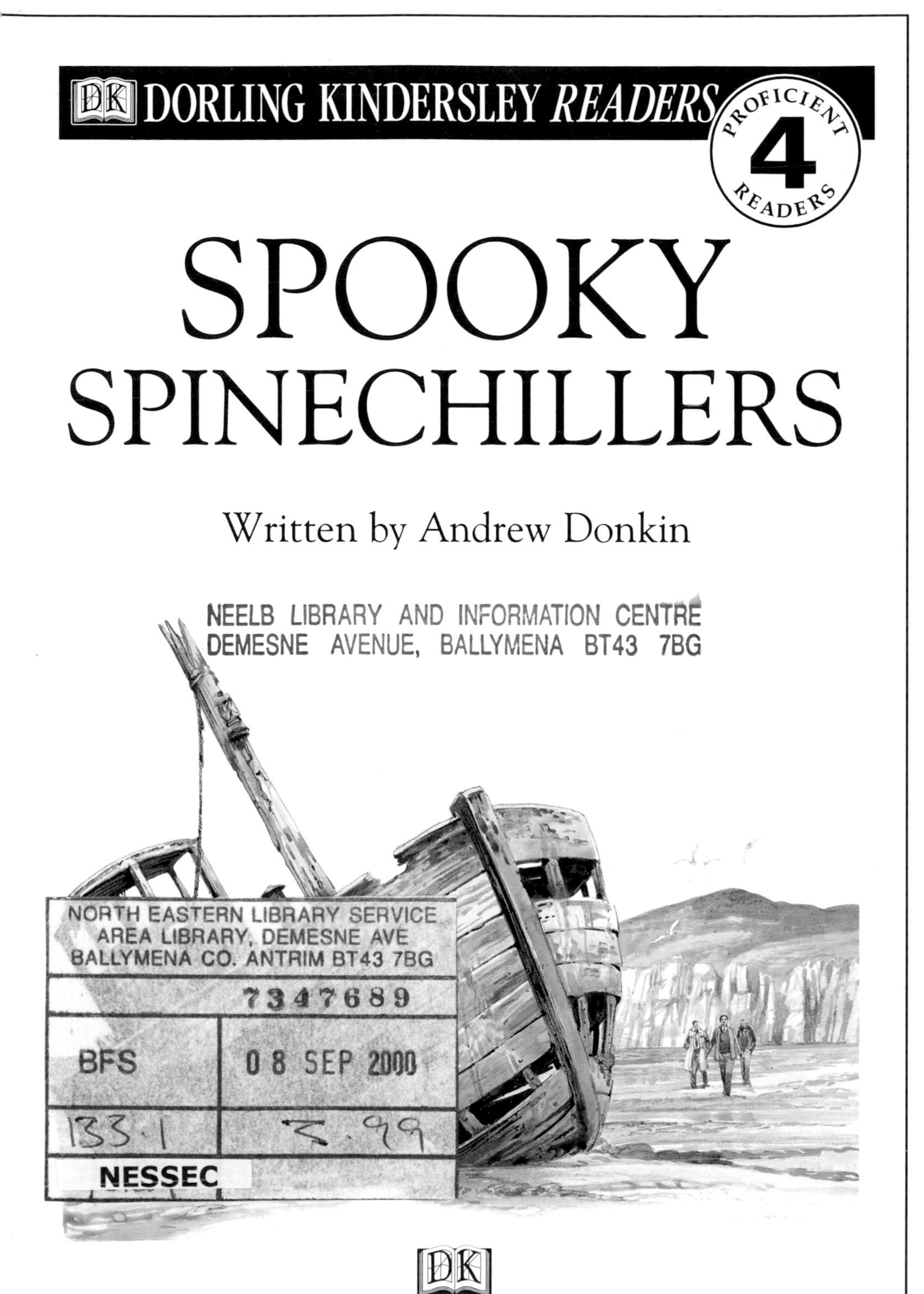

DK
London • New York • Sydney • Delhi
Paris • Munich • Johannesburg

Trick or treat
The traditional time for ghosts to walk the Earth is Hallowe'en, on 31 October. That's when the veil between this world and the supernatural is said to be at its thinnest.

Old haunts
The earliest recorded haunted house was in Greece, 2,000 years ago. A figure bound in clanking chains drove away the tenants of a villa in Athens.

Ghosts and spirits

It's nearly midnight. Your friends dare you to go inside a deserted old house that everyone says is haunted. You creep up the front path to the old oak door. You switch on your torch and turn the handle.

The floorboards creak as you walk along the cold, empty hallway. It smells musty, as though no-one has been there for years.

Trying to be brave, you shine your torch on a dusty old portrait. When you wipe away some cobwebs, a pair of evil-looking eyes stare back at you. Wait – did the eyes just move slightly? Perhaps this old house really is haunted.

You might never find yourself in a real-live ghost story like this. But read on to discover seven incredible ghost stories from around the world. They all have something in common – they are all absolutely true!

A photo of the ghost of Raynham Hall, Norfolk, England

Castle ghosts
Ireland is full of ancient castles. It is said that Leap Castle, near Munster, has many ghosts, including a foul-smelling beast-man.

Top haunts
Ireland has a long tradition of being one of the most haunted places in the world.

The next victim

Arthur Frewen was lost. The twenty-year-old student was on holiday on the south-east coast of Ireland. He was staying with friends at an army barracks. He had been for a walk but now he could not find his way back. As the sun went down, a gloomy twilight settled over the land.

Arthur wrapped his red scarf around his neck and stumbled on along the path by the coast.

Soon it was dark, but Arthur could just see his way by the light of the moon. At last, after what seemed like hours, he saw a light.

As Arthur got closer, he saw that the light came from a fishing boat moored in a bay. An old man was on the deck, mending a fishing net. Arthur explained that he was lost and the man waved for him to step on board.

Irish spirit
A banshee is a traditional form of Irish spirit. Some people have heard its horrible wailing cries just before a death.

Down in the boat's galley, the fisherman thrust a bowl of hot soup into Arthur's hands. Arthur bolted it down but he felt uncomfortable.

The man watched him, like a farmer might watch a turkey just before Christmas.

When Arthur had finished, the old man showed him to a cabin where he could spend the night. Arthur hung up his red scarf on the back of the door and climbed into the bed. He was exhausted, but each time he dropped off, he woke up suddenly to the unmistakable sound of someone sharpening a knife.

Just after midnight, Arthur woke again with a start. This time he heard footsteps coming towards his door. He climbed out of bed and looked through the keyhole. There, walking towards him, was the old man. In his hand he held a large carving knife. Terrified, Arthur pulled himself out through a small window just as the handle of the cabin door began to turn.

Arthur hid for the rest of the night. He found his way back to the barracks by the light of the next morning's dawn.

Violent ends
Many Irish phantoms seem to be people who have met a violent end. Some people living in north Dublin have seen a butcher walking in his house although someone cut his throat in 1863.

Tasty soup
Arthur said that the soup the old man gave him was potato soup and that, under the circumstances, it wasn't bad.

Schoolteacher
Arthur Frewen later became a schoolteacher and wrote several plays.

Ghost beach
The beach at Doonagore Tower on the south coast of Ireland is said to be haunted by the ghosts of Spanish sailors. Their ship was wrecked there in 1588 and the survivors were murdered by the local sheriff.

Arthur told his friends what had happened and they decided to go back to the boat together. When they reached the bay, they could see only a wreck covered with seaweed. The fishing boat of last night had gone, along with the old man.

"Perhaps you met the Dungarven murderer," said one of Arthur's friends. "This is supposed to be his boat. He lured people aboard and then stabbed them to death with a carving knife. The police arrested him eventually."

"He must have escaped from prison," said Arthur. "We should call the police."

"It's too late for that," said the friend. "He was hung in Dungarven more than 70 years ago. His last victim was a student, just like you."

The blood drained from Arthur's face. How could the old fisherman be dead? He climbed inside the wreck to have a look around. Most of the timbers were rotten and he had to cover his nose to block out the stench of decay. He was just about to leave when something caught his eye. On the back of a door hung his bright red scarf!

Executions
Public hangings often drew a large crowd. The people cheered as the victims were hung by the neck until they were dead.

Creepy cat
In 1968, the ghost of a cat appeared several times to workmen in a house in southern Ireland. The animal was as big as a dog. It terrified all the men with its red and orange eyes.

The phantom pilot

L-1011
A Lockheed L-1011 aircraft is also known as a Tristar airbus.

Just before midnight on 29 December, 1972, Eastern Airlines Flight 401 fell out of the sky. The Lockheed L-1011 plunged to earth and crashed in the Everglades area of Florida, USA.

Of the 176 people on board, 99 died, including the aircraft's captain, Bob Loft, and the flight engineer, Don Repo. The terrible accident shocked everyone in the country and cast a shadow over the whole of Eastern Airlines.

Evening News
Helicopter nets scoop up survivors from TriStar disaster
GIANT JET CRASHES IN SWAMP: 80 DIE

Bad news
The crash of Flight 401 was reported all over the world.

About three months after the crash, a high-ranking executive of Eastern Airlines boarded an aircraft for Miami, Florida. He spotted a man in captain's uniform sitting alone in the first-class section and went to sit down beside him.

The executive struck up a conversation with the captain. After a few minutes he realized that he was talking to Bob Loft. Then the captain faded away.

Flying time
The plane used during Flight 401 had completed a total of nearly 1,000 hours in the air and more than 500 safe landings.

Premonition
Doris Elliot, a crew member with Eastern Airlines, had a vision of the crash a month before it happened. She dreamed of a plane crashing at night in the Everglades. She even foretold the week of the terrible crash.

A week later, an Eastern Airlines captain and two of his crew went into a staffroom at John F Kennedy Airport, in New York. They all saw Bob Loft in a chair. He talked to them for a while, then vanished. The men were so shocked that the airline had to cancel their flight.

Three weeks after that incident, a woman was sitting in the first-class section of a flight to Miami. She was worried about the man in an Eastern Airlines uniform sitting next to her. His face was white and he looked ill, so she called over one of the cabin crew.

She leaned down to speak to the man but he ignored her. Then, as she touched his arm, he slowly faded away, leaving only an empty seat.

When the plane landed in Miami, the woman was taken to a hospital in a state of shock. Later, when she saw photographs, she identified the ghost as flight engineer Don Repo.

Witnesses
There have been more recorded sightings of the ghosts of Flight 401 than of any other ghost.

Safe travel
In the USA, fewer people have died in air crashes in the past 60 years than die in car accidents in a typical three-month period.

Phantom flyer
Another ghostly pilot has been seen by visitors and workers at the Castle Air Force Museum in California, USA. The spook haunts the cabin of a Second-World-War aircraft on display in the museum.

Over the next few months, more than 10 airline staff claimed to have seen Don Repo. Once, he appeared to men loading food onto an aircraft. They fled in terror.

On another occasion, he warned a crew to watch out for fire on their aircraft. When fire broke out in one of the engines, the crew was ready and dealt with the fire quickly.

The ghost of Don Repo seemed to appear more often on some aircraft than on others. Rumours began to spread that all the planes on which he had appeared had replacement parts taken from the crashed Flight 401. It is usual practice for an airline to use undamaged parts from a crashed plane in another plane if they pass strict safety tests.

The stories must have worried the bosses of Eastern Airlines. They ordered their engineers to remove from their planes all equipment salvaged from the 401 wreck.

It seemed to work – when all the 401 parts had been removed, Bob Loft and Don Repo left Eastern Airlines and their aircraft in peace. No-one has seen their ghosts since.

Runway ghost
A man in a bowler hat haunts a runway at Heathrow Airport in London. He stands on the spot where his plane crashed in 1948.

In print
The journalist John Fuller investigated the ghosts of Flight 401 and uncovered the evidence about the replaced parts. He wrote a best-selling book that told the story.

Adventure
In 1911, Charlotte Moberley and Eleanor Jourdain published an account of their walk in Versailles. It was called *An Adventure.*

A walk in the past

On a hot afternoon in 1901, Charlotte Moberley and Eleanor Jourdain set out from their apartment in Paris, France. They were going to visit the Palace of Versailles, which had been the home of the French royal family until 1789.

The two women wanted to see the Petit Trianon, a small palace in the grounds of the main one.

French palace
The French king Louis XIV started the building of the Palace of Versailles in 1661, on the site of a royal hunting lodge. It was finished in 1756.

As Charlotte and Eleanor reached the Petit Trianon, they both noticed a change in atmosphere. They felt as if they were walking into a blanket of silence. Everything was flat and distant.

The women saw gardeners working in the flowerbeds. They all wore old-fashioned clothes – strange three-sided hats and long coats.

Royal gift
The Petit Trianon was built in 1774 by Louis XVI as a gift to his wife, Marie Antoinette.

Horse and cart
When Elizabeth Hatton visited the palace of Versailles in 1948, she saw an old-style horse and cart that suddenly vanished.

Eleanor and Charlotte continued their walk but began to feel sad. As they walked towards the palace, Charlotte saw a woman in a white dress sitting on a seat. She looked exactly like Marie Antoinette.

Marie Antoinette in the Trianon park, *a painting by Antoine Vestier*

As the women entered the palace everything seemed normal again and they continued their visit.

Some days later, the friends discussed their trip to Versailles. Charlotte was amazed to discover that Eleanor had not seen the woman on the lawn although she had walked straight past her.

Eleanor returned to the Petit Trianon some months later. There were far more trees than she remembered, and some of the paths that she had walked along with Charlotte were now blocked by brick walls. She asked a guide why the walls had been built so suddenly.

The guide looked surprised at her question. "The walls have been there for more than 100 years," he told her.

Eleanor and Charlotte were sure that when they visited Versailles, they had stepped back into the past.

Revolution
Between 1789 and 1795, a revolution took place in France. It ended the monarchy and France became a republic. Louis XVI and Marie Antoinette were beheaded.

Into the past
In 1916, Edith Oliver walked around a fairground in the small English village of Avebury. She later discovered that the last fair was held there in 1850!

Poltergeists
These noisy, invisible spirits are known for throwing things violently around a room.

Supernatural
The Reverend Foyster was the third vicar to try to live in Borley Rectory. All the families experienced strange things and had to move out.

Ghosthunter

Strange things were happening at Borley Rectory in England. Moans and whispers came from the walls. Plates and candlesticks flew through the air. The Reverend Smith and his wife needed help.

On 12 June, 1929, Britain's number one ghostbuster, Harry Price, arrived at the rectory. He was a psychic investigator who collected and recorded scientific evidence of the supernatural.

Price set himself up in the study with his ghost-hunting kit. He had cameras and tape recorders for recording strange images and sounds, as well as torches and candles so he could see things moving in the dark.

Price sealed the door with tape. He dusted the floor with flour to pick up footprints and put a bowl of mercury on the table to detect ghostly tremors. He then set up movement-sensitive alarms to wake him if a ghost stirred.

But none of this equipment stopped an invisible presence from locking the study door from inside without Price noticing.

No tricks
Harry Price tried to expose fakes. Before he started work in a house, he made sure that everyone was accounted for. He often locked them in a room and sealed the door with tape.

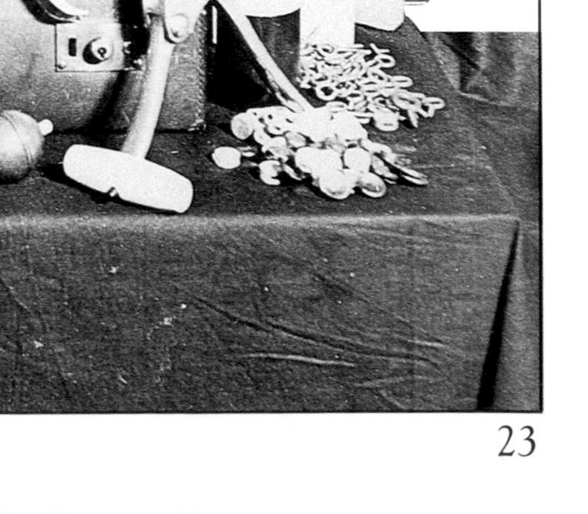

Harry Price was fascinated by Borley Rectory and declared it to be "the most haunted house in England". He rented the house for a year and moved in a team of researchers. The team carefully noted everything they saw.

During the investigations, Price discovered that one ghost appeared again and again. It was the ghost of a nun, and since 1885 at least ten people had seen her in her flowing robes. Price looked into the Borley records and learned of a tragic local legend. In the 11th century, when a monastery stood on the site of the rectory, a young nun and a monk fell in love. They tried to run away together but were caught. The monk was beheaded and the nun was walled up and left to die.

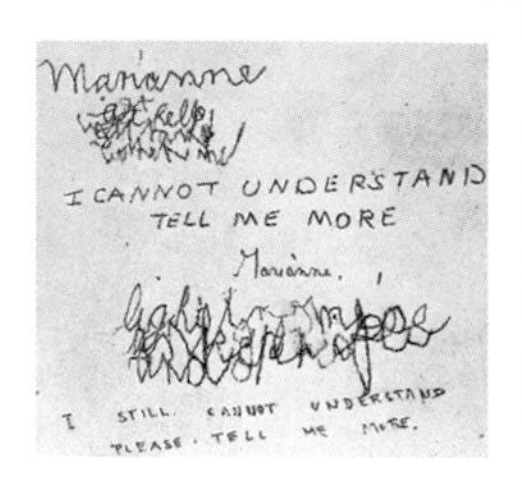

Ghost writing
Writing often appeared on the walls of the rectory. A spirit seemed to want to contact Marianne, the Reverend Foyster's wife.

Church ghosts
Nearby Borley Church is also supposed to be haunted. Villagers have heard ghostly footsteps and the organ has played music when no one was sitting at it.

Price's technical equipment failed to help him find out more about the nun so he decided to contact the spirits directly. He made a planchette – a small, heart-shaped board on wheels with a pencil pushed through it. He placed it on a sheet of paper, rested his hand on it, and waited for the Borley ghosts to contact him and guide his hand.

Ancient site
Borley Rectory was built by Henry Bull in 1863 on the spot where a manor house once stood. The manor had existed as long ago as 1066 and had been built on the site of an ancient monastery.

Borley ghosts
The ghosts of Borley Rectory include a large dog and a carriage drawn by some jet-black horses.

After a while, the planchette began to move. It confirmed on the paper that long ago, a nun had been murdered in the monastery. It also predicted that a fire would destroy the rectory and that someone would discover the body of the nun beneath the ruins.

As predicted, Borley Rectory burned to the ground in 1939. Harry Price dug up the cellar to see if the spirits of the planchette had been right about the nun too. It wasn't long before his shovel hit something. He leaned down and brushed away the dirt. There was the skull of a young woman. It had to be the nun's!

Price arranged for the bones to be buried in a nearby churchyard, but the spirits did not rest. The ghostly shadow of a young woman in long flowing robes still haunts the old grounds of the rectory.

Harry's return
Price may have appeared as a ghost to a man in hospital. The patient saw him at his bedside.

Flaming ghosts
Tiny flames sometimes shimmer in marshes. They are caused by burning gases from the rotting plants. People thought that they were ghosts and called them will-o'-the-wisps.

Raising spirits
Monks in Tibet believe that they can create a spirit by concentrating. The spirits are called tulpas and can be good or evil.

Flames of the dead

It was a hot night in June, 1907. Peter Smith, an officer in the cavalry, was asleep in his army cottage in Delhi, India. Suddenly, he woke with a jolt. He sat up and looked at his watch. It was 2.30 am. On the wall around his bed, he saw the reflection of flames. Someone must be having a bonfire outside. Why were they doing it so late?

Smith got up and went to the window. The lawn outside was empty. There was no sign of any fire. Puzzled, Smith went back to bed. As he drifted into a restless sleep, the flames still danced across his wall.

On the following night, Smith woke up at exactly the same time. Again, the reflection of flames flickered across his white bedroom wall. They seemed even brighter than before.

The same thing happened on the third night. Then, on the fourth night, the flames were larger than ever. This time Smith could hear the crackle of a fire outside. Once again, he got out of bed. Although it was another hot night, he shivered as he went over to the window to investigate.

Protection
Many people in India believe that ghosts are evil spirits and are dangerous. Some people arrange piles of small stones and place food and drink inside for the ghosts. They hope the ghosts will then leave them alone.

Annual ghosts
Some ghosts appear only on a certain day each year. US President Lincoln was murdered in 1865. The ghost of the train that took his body home is often seen on the anniversary of his death.

Smith rubbed his eyes. This time there was someone out there. He could see two soldiers dragging something across the lawn towards a blaze of flames. Smith went to find out what they were doing but, as he walked towards them, they and the bonfire vanished in front of his eyes.

Smith thought that he must have been having a dream. The next day, he told his dream to a fellow officer.

"Your dream sounds like something that happened here 50 years ago," said the officer and he told Smith the story.

"Two cavalry soldiers murdered their commanding officer and his wife in a cottage that stood just next door to yours. At 2.30 am in the morning, they dragged the bodies across the lawn, then burned them just outside your window. It happened on a hot night in June."

Ghostbusters
In India, if a family is pestered by an evil spirit, they may pay a person called a shaycana to come and scare away the spook.

Nightlife
Las Vegas is a large city in Nevada. It is famous for its gambling casinos and night spots.

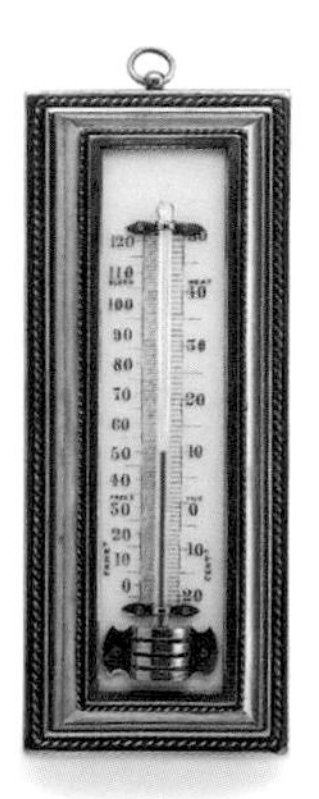

Cold spots
In many reports of hauntings, people describe feeling a sudden drop in temperature before they see the ghost.

The uninvited guest

When Hilary Spence returned to Las Vegas, USA, from a holiday in England, she took home a small cottage made of pottery. It was a present from her aunt and had been in the family for years. Her aunt had kept postage stamps in it and Hilary decided to keep stamps inside it too. She put the cottage on a shelf in her kitchen.

After a few days, Hilary noticed a change in the atmosphere in her house. She saw dark shadows appear out of nowhere and move around the room. Areas of the kitchen suddenly became icy cold.

One night, Hilary was clearing up in the kitchen when, out of the corner of her eye, she saw something move. She turned to look.

There, in the corner of the kitchen, was a tall man wearing a top hat and old-fashioned clothes. He walked straight past Hilary and through the kitchen door. Then he vanished.

Through walls
Many ghosts seem to be able to walk straight through walls and doors. This may be because the wall or door through which they walk was not there when they were alive.

Screen ghost
In 1984, the spirit of a man called Harden sent messages via a computer. He wrote in old English, as it was used hundreds of years ago.

London Bridge
Engineers took down the original London Bridge over the River Thames and rebuilt it in Arizona, USA. It is said that some of the bridge's ghosts went with it.

Hilary was certain that she had seen a ghost and thought that he must be linked to the shadows and the cold spots. She wondered if he had come to her house with the little cottage, because they both appeared at the same time.

When her daughter, Billie, came to visit her, Hilary told her about the cottage. Billie loved a good ghost story and was fascinated by the pottery cottage. She decided to take it home with her and put it in her own kitchen.

Very soon, Billie noticed dark menacing shadows moving across the walls. It was as if an invisible person had entered her house.

Then one night, just after midnight, Billie lay in bed thinking about the cottage. Suddenly, she heard footsteps in the corridor. She crept out of bed and slowly opened her door. Nervously, she looked out.

A tall man in old-fashioned clothes stood on the landing. He looked just like the man that her mother had described to her. Before Billie could speak, he faded away into nothing.

Stop the clock
It is curious that many clocks have stopped at the exact moment when their owners died.

Star mirror
Movie star Marilyn Monroe is said to haunt a mirror that she owned. Marilyn died suddenly on 4 August, 1962.

Billie sensed that the ghost was unhappy but she did not know why. Maybe he did not like her mother's stamps that were still inside the cottage. She took the stamps out and put in different things instead. First she tried money, then her collection of pens and pencils, but the shadows continued to appear. She swapped the pens for biscuits but that didn't work either. The ghost still seemed to be unhappy.

Billie ran out of things to put inside the cottage and decided to leave it empty. Immediately, the strange atmosphere in the house lifted. Billie knew that at last the ghost was happy, now that he had the cottage to himself.

Since then, Billie has not seen any more strange shadows. Neither has she seen the tall man in the top hat. The little cottage is still in her kitchen. It's empty, of course. Or is it?

Spices
The export of spices from India to Europe and America was called the Spice Trade. Spices come from plants and are used for flavouring food. Cinnamon and ginger are spices.

Ginger root

Cinnamon sticks

Seaport
In the early 20th century, Bombay was one of the largest ports in India. The traders piled up their goods on the dock.

The last command

"Fire! Fire!" shouted the terrified seaman at the top of his voice. He ran up from the ship's hold, followed by a cloud of thick, black smoke. It was 1902 and the sailing ship *Firebird* was three days away from Bombay in India. A storm was brewing and the sea was rough. An oil lamp had overturned in the hold, setting fire to a bag of spices.

The blaze spread quickly. Every crew member tried to fight the fire but it was hopeless. One of the tall wooden masts caught alight and the flames licked dangerously at its sails.

"Lower all the lifeboats!" shouted the horrified captain to his men. "Abandon ship!"

As the crew leaped to safety, the ship's mast broke.

"Look out!" a man called, but no one heard him above the roar of the flames. The falling mast struck the captain, killing him instantly. A sailor bravely rescued the captain's body and jumped with it into the sea. Seconds later, the *Firebird* slipped beneath the waves and disappeared forever.

Cursed
The British ship the *Lady Lovibond* seems cursed to repeat its final moments forever. The ghost of the ship has smashed onto the same rocks off the English coast several times since she sank in 1748.

Three kilometres from the fire, another ship, the *James Gilbert*, was sailing away from the storm. A young helmsman was at the wheel.

Suddenly, a man in a captain's uniform appeared before the helmsman. He had a terrible scar down the side of his face. The young man did not know the captain but he stood to attention.

"Change course to north-by-north-west," ordered the captain.

The young sailor hesitated. He knew that the new course would take the *James Gilbert* straight into the storm but it wasn't his place to argue. He always had to obey a captain's order.

The captain of thc *James Gilbert* was in his cabin. When he felt his ship turn he rushed up on deck. "Why have you changed course?" he shouted at the helmsman. "You are heading towards the storm."

The terrified helmsman pointed towards where the scarred captain had been standing. But the stranger was nowhere to be seen.

At that moment, a voice from the crow's nest, high up on the mast, called out, "Lifeboats ahoy!" The *James Gilbert*'s new course had taken her directly into the path of the *Firebird*'s drifting lifeboats.

Sea legend
Many people have seen the famous phantom ship, the *Flying Dutchman*. On 11 July, 1881, King George V of England saw it in the South Atlantic when he was a naval cadet on HMS *Inconstant*.

A warning
While sailing to England on the *Waratah*, in July 1909, Claude Sawyer had a dream in which the ghost of a knight told him the ship would sink. He changed vessels, and shortly afterwards, the *Waratah* was lost at sea.

The storm grew worse and the crew of the *James Gilbert* began to pull the drifting men on board, one by one. The helmsman reached down to help a man in a lifeboat.

"It's a miracle that you sailed this way," said the sailor. "We wouldn't have survived in these lifeboats. Will you help me lift our captain's body on board?"

The helmsman took the body and hauled the dead captain on board.

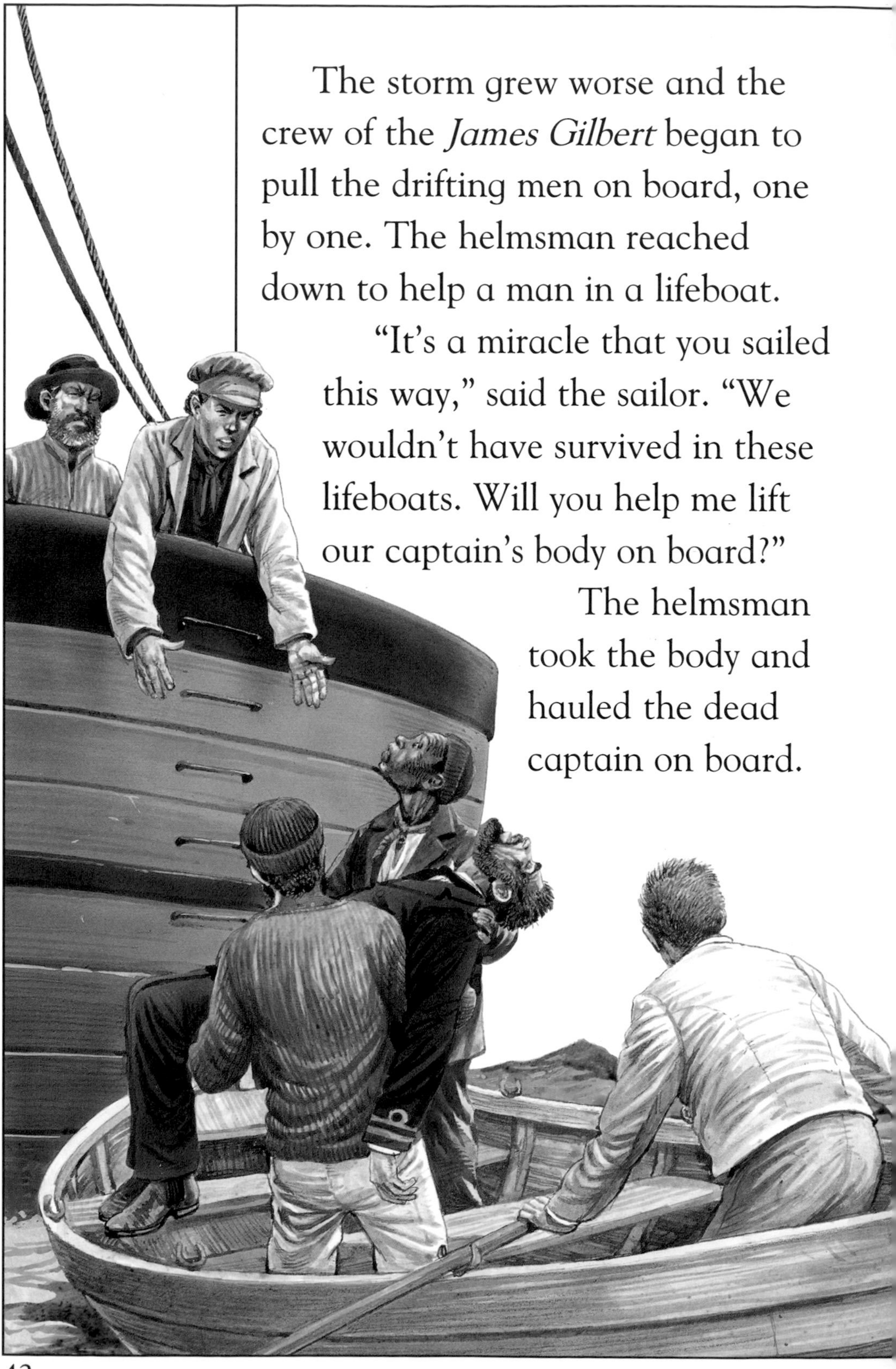

He laid the captain on the deck. It was only then that he noticed a dreadful wound on the side of the man's face. This was the stranger who had ordered him to change course!

The young helmsman staggered backwards, staring at the dead man.

"What's wrong, boy?" asked the captain of the *James Gilbert.* "You look as if you've seen a ghost!"

"I think I have," replied the shaken helmsman.

At last, the *James Gilbert* turned and headed away from the storm. The crew of the *Firebird* was safe, but they knew that if it had not been for their captain they would all have died there in the storm.

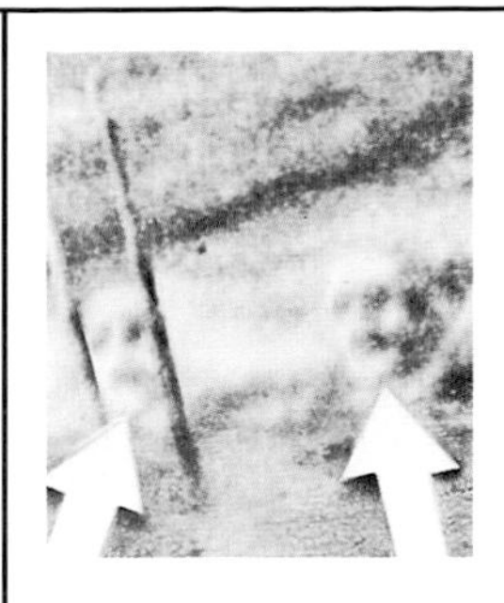

On the waves
In 1929, two dead crew members haunted the SS *Watertown.* Images of the men's faces appeared on the waves. A crew member managed to take this photo.

Rescue mission
A mysterious figure appeared on a British ship in 1828. He wrote "Steer north-west" on a blackboard, then vanished. The captain obeyed the request and was able to save a ship and its crew that was trapped in ice.

What are ghosts?

The traditional explanation of ghosts is that they are the surviving spirits of the dead. There are many different reasons why they haunt the living. Some may want to talk to a friend or relative. Others may not be able to rest because they were murdered, and their killers were never brought to justice.

Some ghosts repeat their actions. Roman soldiers haunt a house in northern England, marching through the cellar time and again. When they appear, half their legs are below the floor. Maybe the Roman road along which they walk is lower than the cellar.

Ancient spirits
"The Epic of Gilgamesh", carved in stone more than 4,000 years ago, is one of the first stories ever recorded that features a ghost.

Black dog
The most common type of animal ghost reported is a black dog.

Most ghosts haunt the places in which they lived when they were alive. In Brittany, France, departed loved ones are said to return to their homes once a year on All Saints' Eve, or Hallowe'en.

Ghost feelings
Some ghosts are not visible. Instead, they create a feeling of unease or sadness around them, or maybe a strange atmosphere.

Le Toussaint *(Hallowe'en), from the magazine* L'Illustration *(1895)*

Fake photograph of Jane Seymour, third wife of King Henry VIII of England

An unusual ghost is one that speaks. Some people were skiing near Oslo, Norway, when a woman ordered them off her land. When she vanished, the skiers realized that they had been told off by a ghost.

Many people do not believe in ghosts. They think that anyone who says that they have seen a ghost has an overactive imagination. They explain the "ghosts" as optical illusions and tricks of the light.

Some ghosts are known to be hoaxes. This photograph is supposed to show the ghost of Jane Seymour at Hampton Court near London, but tests have proved that it is a fake.

There are lots of sightings of ghosts that cannot be explained. All the major religions of the world believe in life after death, so isn't it possible that some spirits roam the Earth? They may be all around you now – you just can't see them.

Scented ghosts
Some ghosts are associated with a smell. The headless ghost of a lady in Bovey House, England, always smells of lavender.

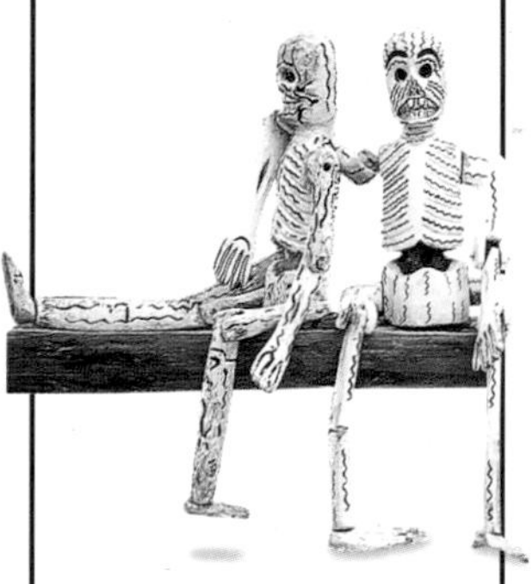

Ghost parties
At the Day of the Dead festival in Mexico, people invite the spirits of dead friends and relatives to a party. They decorate the town with items such as these wooden figures of skeletons.

Glossary

Atmosphere
A good or bad feeling a person might get about a particular place.

Cold spot
A small area of intense cold that is often reported by witnesses during a ghost sighting.

Crow's nest
The top of a ship's mast where the ship's lookout stood to keep watch.

Execution
The lawful killing of a criminal as punishment for crimes committed.

Fake
Something that looks real but has been created to fool people.

Ghost
The spirit of a dead person seen on Earth.

Ghostbuster
A person who helps people to get rid of ghosts or spirits.

Hallowe'en
The night of 31 October, when spirits are said to walk the Earth.

Helmsman
A person who stands at the wheel of a ship and controls and steers it.

Hoax
A trick played to make people believe something that is not true.

Hold
The large area inside a ship's hull where cargo is stored during a voyage.

Hunting lodge
A small building in the countryside where people stay during a hunting trip.

Manor house
A large building with grounds belonging to a nobleman.

Monarchy
A government of a country of which there is a hereditary head of state, such as a king.

Monastery
A house where monks live and worship.

Old English
The type of English spoken centuries ago during the Middle Ages.

Optical illusion
An effect that deceives the brain into thinking it sees something else.

Phantom
Another word for a ghost or spirit.

Planchette
A device that some people believe can be used to talk to spirits.

Poltergeist
An invisible spirit said to throw objects around and make strange noises.

Psychic investigator
An expert who probes supernatural mysteries.

Rectory
A house near a church where the priest lives.

Revolution
A complete change in government or conditions, often caused by a people's uprising.

Shaycana
An Indian expert on the supernatural who keeps away evil spirits.

Spirit
The part of a person that is said to go on existing after the body dies.

Supernatural
Anything that cannot be explained by science – especially ghosts and haunted houses.

Trick or treat
Tradition of Hallowe'en, when children threaten to play a trick on their neighbours unless they are given a sweet.

Vision
A sudden glimpse of an event or place that is not in front of the observer's eyes.

Will-o'-the-wisps
Bluish flames seen in swamps and marshes. They were once thought to be spirits but are really burning marsh gas.